"Stop giggling!"

The light on the camera flashed.

Amy smiled. That photo of her little sister was going to look really wicked.

# Make Friends With
# Amy

# Ann Bryant

ORCHARD BOOKS

# Chapter One

"Shopping, you two! Five minutes! Make sure you're ready. I haven't got any time to waste!"

Amy was lying on top of the wardrobe, squeezed into the tiny space under the ceiling. She was looking through the window in her camera. "OK, stand still, Sabrina!" she said to her little sister. "It sounds like Dad means business!"

Sabrina giggled.

"And stop giggling."

The light on the camera flashed. Amy smiled. She was pleased with her idea of climbing up on the wardrobe to take the photo looking down at Sabrina. It was going to look really wicked.

"Amy!" her dad called upstairs, "Can you look in the bathroom and see if we need loo paper or toothpaste or anything?"

Amy sighed and started to lower herself off the wardrobe on to the chair. "You'd better get changed, Sabrina. I think Dad might be a bit embarrassed walking round the supermarket with you looking like that."

"No he won't. He'll like it, because all the people will say, 'Oh look at that little girl! I think she ought to be a supermodel when she grows up!'"

Amy laughed. Sabrina had dressed up

brilliantly to have her photo taken, but it wasn't all that brilliant for going shopping. She'd put her vest on top of her pyjama top and poked a piece of green ribbon through the armholes of the vest, then she'd tied the ribbon in front, in a tight knot with the ends dangling down. On her bottom half she was wearing a pair of Amy's blue winter woollen tights, which were miles too big for her and made wrinkles all down her thin little legs. On top of that she'd wrapped a scarf of their dad's round and round her middle as a sort of short skirt. But it looked more like a colourful bulky nappy. And on her feet was a pair of their mum's best high-heeled shoes.

"Well, at least change the tights," said Amy. "And hurry up about it."

As Amy went off to her own room to

put her socks and trainers on, she heard her dad calling out, "Are you ready, you two?"

"Coming," called Amy.

And a few seconds later she was sliding down the banister.

"Where's Sabrina?" asked her dad, who was standing in the hall, frowning and looking impatient.

"She's just changing. She won't be a min—"

The words froze on Amy's lips as she and her dad watched a grinning Sabrina tottering downstairs. She hadn't changed at all. She'd just made herself worse by backcombing her fine light brown hair into a terrible sticking up tangly mess that looked like a bird's nest left over from last year. She'd also smeared loads of grey eyeshadow all over her lips, so she looked like something frightening that might jump out at you if you were on a ghost train.

"Please let this be a bad dream," mumbled their dad, as he shook his head in amazement.

"Go and get changed!" said Amy crossly.

Now I sound just like Mum, she thought to herself. It must be because Mum's away at Granny's. It makes me feel as though *I'm* the one in charge of Sabrina.

"I haven't got time to wait for her to get changed," said their dad, crossly. "You'll just have to come as you are, Sabrina." He sighed impatiently and looked at his watch. "I must be back before lunch. I'm expecting an important business call."

"She'll break her leg trying to walk in Mum's shoes…"

"What! Mum's shoes!" Her dad shot upstairs two at a time. "Come on!" he said, scooping Sabrina up and carting her downstairs like a sack of potatoes. "Take the shoes off her feet," he instructed Amy, a bit snappily, just before they went out of the front door.

"No!" squealed Sabrina, trying to wriggle her way out of her dad's arms. "I love these shoes."

Amy saw Sabrina's wellies by the front door so she grabbed them, and they all got into the car.

"I look stupid in these wellies!" whined Sabrina from her booster seat in the back.

"Your wellies are the only normal thing you've got on!" laughed Amy.

"Take that vest off her," said their dad to Amy. "That should improve things a bit!"

Amy was quite surprised, because Sabrina didn't try to stop her. She sat perfectly still, her chin stuck up in the air, like a queen sitting on a throne.

But it was impossible to get the vest off without undoing the tight knot of the green ribbon. And after a couple of minutes fiddling with it, Amy understood why Sabrina hadn't struggled at all. She'd known perfectly well that Amy wouldn't be able to do it.

"She'll just have to stay like it until we get home, then we'll cut it," said their dad, sighing.

He pulled up in the supermarket car park and out they all piled. It was the school holidays so there were loads of

children about. Unfortunately, a couple
of boys of about Amy's age were getting
out of a car just near Amy's dad's. When
they saw Sabrina they both pointed and
sniggered. Amy pulled a face at them.
But then she took another look at
Sabrina, and felt just a teeny bit anxious.
After all she couldn't go round the
supermarket pulling faces at *everyone* who
laughed at Sabrina, could she?

# Chapter Two

"See!" whispered Sabrina to Amy, her eyes sparkling as they went down the first aisle. "I was right! Everyone's staring at me because they think I look like a supermodel."

Their dad strode on ahead pushing the trolley and frowning at the list he'd made. "Hold Amy's hand, Sabrina," he called back to her.

Amy wasn't too sure about that. Normally she wouldn't care two hoots what her little sister looked like. But today, she had to admit, Sabrina had gone a bit over the top. To make it even worse, she was smiling at all the shoppers. Only it wasn't her usual smile. She was obviously trying to imitate a pop star or something, because she was opening her mouth as wide as it would go and making her lips curl right back. She looked like an alien. But you could tell *she* thought she looked great.

"I don't think Daddy realises what Mummy usually buys," she suddenly told Amy in a very grown-up voice.

"Yes, he does," said Amy, doing a quick count up of how many days were left until their mum would be back from visiting their granny in Wales. Only six and a half, thank goodness.

"Mummy told me she wanted Daddy

to make sure he bought plenty of chocolate biscuits, actually," went on Sabrina. "I'm going to find them."

She went skipping off and Amy suddenly felt very excited because she realised she was the only one in the aisle. She went back a few steps, checked that no one was watching, then did a big run-up that finished in a lovely long slide.

But uh-oh! A girl and her mother were coming round the corner, and Amy couldn't stop herself in time. She knocked into the girl and made her lose her balance for a second.

"Whoops! Sorry!"

The girl didn't say *that's all right* or anything. She just gave Amy a look as if to say, *Clumsy thing!*

"Sorry," said Amy again, going a bit

pink, then she quickly went off to catch up with her dad.

He was by the chocolate biscuits, trying to stop Sabrina putting lots of packets into the trolley.

"What about a nice ride?" he asked her.

Amy knew that Sabrina hadn't had a ride in a supermarket trolley for about two years.

"I'm not a baby, Dad," said Sabrina. "I wouldn't even fit in there!"

"Come on, it'll be fun!" said her dad, lifting her up.

But Sabrina started kicking her legs and one of her wellies came flying off and only just missed an old man who was walking past. Instead it hit the cans of beans behind him and sent a few of them rolling into the aisle.

"Whoops!" said Sabrina, giggling, and wriggling out of her dad's arms. She put her welly back on, then bent down and started picking up the cans of beans. "Silly me!" she told the old man, who looked at her as though she was completely bonkers.

"Let *me* do that," said their dad, sounding very exasperated.

Amy looked at the trolley and suddenly wished *she* was little enough to fit into it. Well…maybe she was…

"Look, Sabrina," she said, "you *would* fit into the trolley. Even someone as big as me would fit in!"

"You would never!" said Sabrina.

"Yes, I would. Look, I'll get in first. Then *you've* got to get in, OK?"

"OK," said Sabrina.

So Amy climbed in. Even though she

was quite thin it was still almost impossible to get her legs through. Her dad was picking up the last tin of beans when Sabrina suddenly spotted a little girl at the end of the aisle, dragging along a pretend dog on a lead.

"Oh sweet!" said Sabrina, rushing off.

"Come back!" called her dad, turning round just in time to see her disappearing round the end of the aisle. He ran after her and Amy was left stuck with one leg in and one leg out of the trolley. She felt a complete idiot, especially when she found she really was stuck, and all she could do was to wait for her dad to get back.

And that was when the girl who Amy had crashed into came round the corner. She gave Amy a quick glance, then totally ignored her and started looking at all the different cereals on the shelves.

Now she thinks I'm clumsy *and* crazy! thought Amy crossly. And she would have kicked the trolley if she'd had a leg free to do it.

# Chapter Three

"Can you get me out of here!" said Amy crossly, when her dad appeared a moment later, holding Sabrina's hand. Sabrina's bottom lip was trembling, so she'd obviously had a big telling-off from their dad. Good. Amy felt like wringing her neck.

Their dad laughed when he saw Amy, and then she felt like wringing *his* neck too. At least that snooty girl had gone. She'd acted like she hadn't even noticed that someone was stuck half in and half out of a trolley. She'd just grabbed a packet of cereal and walked straight past Amy with her nose in the air. Amy had waited a few seconds, then turned round to see if the girl was looking. And she had been, so Amy had pulled a face because she was so cross about being stuck in the trolley.

It was quite a struggle getting out of the trolley. But now Amy was standing on the ground once more she wished she hadn't pulled that face. What if the girl told her mum, and her mum told Amy off in front of lots of people?

The rest of the time in the supermarket was like a game of hide-and-seek.

"There's a snooty girl walking round with her mum," said Amy to Sabrina. "She's wearing a blue top. Whisper to me if you see her, OK?"

Sabrina nodded as she peeped round the next aisle. Then she beckoned Amy with her hand, as though they were escaping the baddies in a gangster film.

It worked very well until they got to the checkout.

"Amy!" hissed Sabrina in a loud whisper. "There's that snooty girl you didn't want to see!"

Amy clapped her hand over Sabrina's mouth and shot a quick glance at their dad to see if he'd heard. But he was paying the bill and didn't seem to have noticed anything. Out of the corner of her eye, Amy could see that the girl's mum was busy putting their shopping into bags at the next checkout. But the girl was staring straight ahead and she'd gone rather red.

✿ ✿ ✿

The next day, Amy's friend, Jade, was coming to play. Amy couldn't wait for two o'clock to arrive. Sabrina was really excited too because she'd got a friend called Lizzy coming round.

Amy was emptying the dishwasher in the kitchen, while her dad made himself a cup of coffee. Any minute now he'd go into his little office by the living room. He'd worked at home for as long as Amy could remember. Only this week, since Amy and Sabrina's mum had been away, he'd not got much done.

"You'll be able to do some work this afternoon, won't you, Dad?" said Amy.

"Let's hope so," said her dad, giving her a wink. "You'll come and tell me if Sabrina and Lizzy get up to anything naughty, won't you?"

Amy nodded. "I hope I get invited back to Jade's house. I love going there. It's much quieter than here."

"Well, I'll let you into a secret," said Amy's dad, with a wink. "*I* hope you get invited back there too! In fact Friday would be ideal."

"Why Friday?"

"Because I've got a business lunch in town on Friday, and I'd completely forgotten Mum wouldn't be here when I arranged it. Still, never mind…"

"Couldn't me and Sabrina come for lunch too? We'd be good as gold. Honestly."

Her dad laughed. "You're joking!" He poured out his coffee. "You never know, maybe Sabrina will get invited back to Lizzy's." Her dad suddenly frowned. "And talking of Sabrina,

24

where *is* she right now?"

"In her room, I think. She was tidying out her drawers as a surprise for Mum."

"Wonders will never cease!" laughed her dad.

And then there was a scratching noise, followed by a bang as though something had dropped on the floor very nearby.

"What's that?" said Amy, feeling alarmed.

Her dad rolled his eyes, so Amy knew straight away what it was.

"I think there must be an extra big mouse in our cupboard, Ames."

"What, Supermouse?" giggled Amy.

And out of the tall cupboard, where they kept the cleaning things, popped Sabrina, flinging the door open so it banged against the wall. She was grinning all over her face. "I've been hiding from you for ages!"

"Lucky you!" said Amy, rolling her eyes back at her dad. She liked it when she and her dad exchanged secret looks about Sabrina. It made her feel really grown-up.

The next moment the doorbell rang and Sabrina shot off to answer it, yelling, "Supermouse in action!"

# Chapter Four

Amy and Jade had a brilliant afternoon together. Most of the time they were up in Amy's bedroom. They were only disturbed twice by Sabrina. Both times it was because she and Lizzy were trying to sneak in and pinch Amy's camera. It had been her best birthday present, and she didn't want Sabrina getting her hands on it.

"Why don't you say that you'll take a photo of them later if they leave us alone for a while?" suggested Jade.

So that's what Amy did. And it was a good idea because the younger ones spent the next twenty minutes getting dressed up in weird clothes for the photo. Then Amy thought of letting them use her glittery nail varnish, which took another twenty minutes.

Later, their dad made them tea. He turned a paper napkin into a funny chef's hat and put it on his head. And he put a tea towel over his arm and pretended to be a posh waiter.

"Would Madam care for more beans?" he asked Lizzy, who collapsed in giggles.

"What about a little more apple juice, Madam?" he asked Jade.

By the end of their tea all four girls had laughed so much their tummies hurt. So then they watched a video.

Amy was hoping that Lizzy's mum would arrive first, but when the doorbell rang it was Jade's mum.

"Can Amy come back to our house on Friday?" Jade asked her mum straight away.

Amy held her breath. She'd told Jade about her dad's business lunch, and Jade had said she was sure it would be OK for Amy to come over.

"Not on Friday, I'm afraid, love. We've got Uncle Billy's birthday, remember?"

So that was that.

About five minutes later Lizzy's mum turned up.

"Hello Sally," said Sabrina, who got to the door just ahead of everyone else. "Dad was wondering if I could come for lunch on Friday?"

29

"Sabrina! That's rude!" said her dad.

"Well you *were* wondering!" said Sabrina. "I heard you talking to Amy when I was hiding in the kitchen cupboard. And Amy wanted Jade's mummy to invite Amy and then you could meet that man. Only Jade's mummy said no, didn't she?"

Amy thought her dad was looking more embarrassed than she'd ever seen him before. But Lizzy's mum was laughing.

"Kids!" she said, rolling her eyes. "No really, it would be lovely to have Sabrina on Friday...*and* Amy."

"That's really kind of you," said Amy's dad, grinning from ear to ear.

Amy just about managed a smile, but she couldn't wait for Sally and Lizzy to go, so she could throttle her little sister.

It was going to be so boring at Sally's with only two little girls to play with, for hours and hours.

# Chapter Five

On Thursday morning Amy's dad told her that he'd got some good news. The man he was supposed to be meeting for lunch the next day, had phoned up to say that he'd have to cancel it because he'd got to look after his daughter.

"So why is that good news, Dad?"

"Because it turns out that Geoff's daughter – she's called Hannah – is nine years old, just like you! And Geoff and I suddenly thought we might as well get the two of you together. So I've asked him to bring Hannah round here. I thought you'd prefer that, to going to Sally's."

Amy couldn't help feeling excited at the thought of being able to play with someone of her own age, rather than be stuck with the little ones for hours. But she still felt anxious. What if she didn't like Geoff's daughter? Or worse, what if the girl didn't like *her*?

"Wh…what's Geoff's daughter like?"

Amy's dad laughed. "I've no idea, Ames, but let me think…" Still grinning to himself, he rubbed his chin thoughtfully. "Yes, I think Geoff did say that she turned into a goat at exactly twelve thirty every day. So you'll have to watch out for that camera of yours because she might just eat it up. You

33

know what goats are like!"

"Stop it, Dad!" said Amy, but she couldn't help laughing. "What time are they coming?"

"Well, now we're not meeting in town, it could be any time. I've suggested eleven thirty. We'll be about an hour and a half, then we can have lunch after they've gone. "

That evening Amy and Sabrina's mum phoned.

"I'm having a girl called Hannah over tomorrow, Mum. I've never met her or anything."

"Yes, Dad told me."

"I hope she likes doing things like obstacles in the garden."

"Well, remember not everyone likes playing those kind of games. She might be the kind of person who prefers to watch a video or something."

"I can't wait till you come home, Mum. Is Granny all right, now?"

"She's miles better than she was. I'll definitely be home on Monday evening, love."

After Amy had put the phone down from talking to her mum it rang again straight away.

Amy's dad answered it, but Amy was right beside him. As she listened to her dad's half of the conversation she worked out exactly who it was and what they were saying.

"Oh, dear! I am sorry to hear that... Yes, there is a lot of it about. No, not at all... It's really not a problem. Don't worry... Yes...yes, all right. Give Lizzy our love... Bye for now." He put the

phone down and turned to Amy. "That was Sally, she says..."

"I can guess," interrupted Amy. "Lizzy is ill so Sabrina can't play there tomorrow." Amy's dad nodded and frowned at the same time.

"It's OK," said Amy, who was secretly rather relieved. "At least if Hannah and I don't get on, we'll have Sabrina there."

Amy's dad laughed. "That's true!"

# Chapter Six

When it was nearly eleven thirty on Friday morning Amy waited by the window for Geoff's car to appear.

"Cuckoo!"

Amy turned round to see Sabrina dressed up in one of their mum's old tops. She'd got it on upside-down though, with her legs through the sleeves, and more green ribbon holding it up. She'd got bare feet like Amy, only hers were covered in nail varnish, where she'd missed her actual toe nails. Amy grinned, then her eyes went straight back to the window because she'd heard a car drawing up.

"They're here!" she yelled to her dad. Then she shot away from the window in case Hannah saw her there. She stood a bit nervously behind her dad as he opened the front door.

Sabrina crawled through her dad's legs at the last minute and greeted the visitors with, "Cuckoo! I'm down here!"

Amy stared in horror at the girl standing beside Geoff. It was the girl from the supermarket – the one Amy had crashed into and pulled a face at! And now she was standing right here on the doorstep. Amy's heart sank so far she thought it would never come back to normal again.

Sabrina jumped up and yanked Amy down so she could whisper in her ear. "It's that snooty girl!"

Amy went red. This felt like the most embarrassing moment of her life. The men didn't hear because they were talking. But it was impossible to tell if Hannah had heard or not. She was staring at the ground.

"It's very nice of you to let Hannah come along," Geoff was saying. "She's been getting more and more excited all morning."

I bet she's not excited now she knows she's got to play with a girl who slides round supermarkets, sits in trolleys and pulls faces, thought Amy, as she slowly straightened up.

"Right, what are you girls going to do while Geoff and I have our meeting?"

39

said Amy's dad. "Watch a video? Dress up? Go out into the garden?"

The two men were smiling away at the girls. They were both beginning to look a bit embarrassed, and no wonder, because neither Amy nor Hannah had said a single word. They were just standing there looking anywhere but at each other.

"Let's go out in the garden," said Sabrina, taking one of Hannah's hands and one of Amy's. "Come on, let's pretend we're only allowed to skip."

Amy felt her cheeks going even redder. Whatever were they going to do for an hour and a half?

"I think we'll just walk, Sabrina."

Out in the garden, Sabrina climbed up the gate that separated the back garden from the side of the house, and sat with one leg on either side of it.

"Do you want to sit on my horsey, Hannah. You can fit two on this gate, can't you, Amy?"

Hannah shook her head.

"Come on," said Sabrina. "It's good fun."

Hannah shook her head even harder.

"Don't you like horsies?" asked Sabrina.

"Yes, but…" Hannah went a bit pink. "I like real ones…"

"Have you got your own pony?" asked Amy.

"Y…yes," said Hannah.

"Well you can still come and try out *my* horsey, can't you?" said Sabrina.

Amy suddenly felt cross. Hannah must think that riding a gate is pathetic, if she'd got her very own pony.

"No! She doesn't want to do that, Sabrina!" she snapped. But it came out even more snappily than she'd meant it to. And Sabrina pouted at her, then got down from the gate and went marching into the house.

Amy really wished she hadn't spoken, because now it was more embarrassing than ever. At least when Sabrina had been there, there was something going on instead of this terrible silence.

# Chapter Seven

"Er…what shall we do?" Amy asked Hannah, her whole body itching to play with a ball or something.

"I don't mind," said Hannah, looking round the garden.

Amy couldn't help staring at the way Hannah's hair bounced around when she turned her head suddenly. It reminded her of one of those shampoo adverts.

"Do you want to play obstacles?" asked Amy. "We could bring the kitchen

43

chairs out here and crawl through them, then climb over the gate and run round the house…" Amy was getting more and more excited at the thought of all the action, "…then you could get in the wheelbarrow and I could push you as far as the tree, and we could time ourselves, then see if we can do it all faster the next time."

Hannah bit her lip. "Could we just watch telly instead?"

Amy remembered what her mum had said on the phone, and tried not to look too fed up. "OK."

So in they went. They sat side by side on the settee. There was a cartoon on. Amy wasn't sure if Hannah was enjoying it at first, but after a bit she started giggling at some of the funny bits. At one point a frog started bouncing on a trampoline and a big grin appeared on its face. It made both girls burst out laughing.

Then they got a shock because there was a flash from across the room. Sabrina had crept in without either of them noticing, ducked down behind the big armchair, then popped up and taken a photo of them laughing.

"That's my camera, Sabrina!" said Amy crossly, jumping up. "You know you're not allowed to use it."

Sabrina ran outside clutching the camera and giggling. Amy chased after her and Hannah followed Amy. When they were right in the middle of the lawn, Sabrina suddenly stopped. Amy crashed into her and fell over, and that made Hannah trip and fall on top of them both.

Somehow Sabrina managed to wriggle out from the bottom and run back into the house, still giggling.

Hannah got up and started brushing herself down. Amy thought she looked worried. She was examining every single bit of her clothes.

"It's only a bit of dirt," said Amy, to try and cheer Hannah up.

"These are very expensive trousers," said Hannah. "And there's green stains from the grass on them too."

"Will your mum be cross?" asked Amy.

"Yes. I'd better go and wash these bits."

Amy thought Hannah was showing off about her expensive trousers, but she led her into the house and upstairs to the bathroom. It felt funny sitting on the edge of the bath, watching Hannah scrubbing away with the nailbrush. It seemed such a lot of trouble for a little bit of dirt and a grass stain.

Hannah saw Amy watching her. "It's only because they cost a lot of money," she said. "I don't want to spoil them."

Amy was getting a bit fed up of hearing how expensive Hannah's clothes were. She decided to tell Hannah about her really expensive bridesmaid's dress. Maybe that would stop her boasting so much.

"I was one of the bridesmaids at my cousin's wedding a few weeks ago," she said. "We wore the most lovely yellow dresses with chokers and everything. And my cousin, Helen, wore a dress made of pure silk! She looked so beautiful."

"I'm never getting married," was all Hannah said.

Amy knitted her eyebrows together. She hadn't been expecting that from Hannah. Now what should they talk about?

"Do you want a drink?"

"Yes please."

So they got some juice from the kitchen and took it up to Amy's room.

"It's nice in here," said Hannah, looking round. "Especially...that." She was pointing to a photo on Amy's chest of drawers of Amy, Sabrina and their mum and dad.

"That's us at Christmas," said Amy, feeling a bit better.

Hannah stared at the picture for a long time, then said, "The frame's lovely too. I'm going to ask for one like that for my birthday."

"When is your birthday?"

"Not for ages and ages."

Hannah looked down and Amy suddenly knew there was something wrong, but she didn't know what it was.

"Shall we go down and watch telly again?"

"OK," said Hannah.

So they watched telly with Sabrina until Amy's dad and Geoff came in to say that they'd finished their work and it was time for Geoff to take Hannah home.

"Bye," said Amy from the front door.

"Thank you for having me," said Hannah politely.

"Pleasure," said Amy's dad. Then he closed the front door and turned to Amy. "So – did you have a good time?"

"Not really. It was quite boring because Hannah didn't want to do anything fun in case she got her expensive clothes messed up. I thought she was showing off a bit, especially when she said she'd got her own pony."

"Her own pony? I don't think she has."

"So why would she say that?"

Amy's dad frowned and looked at the floor for ages.

"What?" said Amy.

"Let's go and make the lunch together, while Sabrina's watching telly," said her dad. "And I'll tell you what Geoff told me. I think it might make you change your mind about Hannah."

# Chapter Eight

"Hannah's mum and dad split up at the beginning of the school holidays. They live in separate houses now. Geoff says that Hannah's really upset about it. They both still love her, of course. But they don't love each other any more."

Amy felt as though her dad had just poured a bucket of cold water over her. She bit her lip as she remembered the way Hannah had stared for so long at the photo of Amy's family.

But then a terrible thought came into Amy's head. "Is that why Mum's gone to Wales without us, even though it's holidays?" she asked in a small voice. "Have you and Mum split up?"

"No, love, we haven't," said her dad. "Mum's just visiting poor old Granny. She would have taken you two with her if Granny hadn't been so ill."

There was a pause while Amy stared into space. Then she asked, "So which house does Hannah live in, her mum's or her dad's?"

"I think she lives mainly with her mum, but she sees her dad a lot too."

"And where does her pony live?" Then Amy suddenly remembered what her dad had said before. "Oh no…she hasn't got a pony, has she?" Amy knitted her eyebrows together. "But I thought that

was why she didn't want to climb up
on the gate and pretend it was a horse…
because a gate's boring when you've
got your own…" Amy stopped because
she'd suddenly thought of something else.
"Maybe…it was nothing to do with
the gate being boring… Maybe she
was worried about getting her trousers
messed up."

Amy's dad nodded thoughtfully.
"Maybe," he said.

Amy was still thinking back to all that
had happened. "And a bit later, Sabrina
accidentally made Hannah and me trip
up and fall down in the garden. And
Hannah got really worried and even
scrubbed the dirty bits on her trousers
with the nailbrush in the bathroom. So
she *must* have been worried."

Amy's dad looked very serious.

"Do Hannah's parents get mad if she gets her clothes messed up, Dad?"

"I'm sure they don't get cross with Hannah. But I guess they argue with each other quite a bit."

Amy pictured Hannah scrubbing away at her dirty trousers. She must have been scared that her parents would argue with each other about *that*. For the first time Amy felt sorry for Hannah. She could still hear Hannah's voice in her head... *It's only because they cost a lot of money.*

And, at that moment, Amy so wished she could go right back to eleven thirty in the morning and start all over again. Only this time she'd be really nice to Hannah, and try to cheer her up. In fact, it would be even better if she could go back to just before the shopping trip, then she wouldn't have pulled that face.

It must have been so awful for poor Hannah when she'd turned up at a strange house with her dad, and had seen Amy standing at the front door.

Just then, Sabrina came crashing into the kitchen, interrupting Amy's thoughts. "What does it mean when the camera does a whirring noise?" she asked, holding Amy's camera right under their dad's nose.

"It means the film is finished," said their dad.

Amy was thinking about Hannah too much to be cross with Sabrina for using up her last photo.

"When can we see the photos?" asked Sabrina, who was standing on her dad's feet, waiting for him to start walking. "I want to see the ones that *I* took."

"We have to get them developed in

town," said their dad. "Off you get, Sabrina. You can help us make lunch."

Amy suddenly remembered the photo that Sabrina had taken of her and Hannah when they'd been laughing at the cartoon. A great idea popped into her head.

"Can we go into town now, Dad? Please? We can be really quick. I want to get the film developed."

Her dad sighed. "Come on, then."

"Brilliant!"

Later that day, Amy sat on her bed with all twenty-four photos spread out on the quilt. It was amazing, but the one that Sabrina had taken was the best. Amy and Hannah looked as though they were really good friends sitting close together and having fun.

56

Very carefully Amy took the picture of her family out of its frame and put the one of her and Hannah in. It was a perfect fit. Next she put the frame with the new picture into the padded envelope that her dad had given her from his office. Then she read through the letter that she'd written to Hannah, before she put it in the envelope.

Dear Hannah,

This present is for you. If you want to play at my house or at one of your houses one day it would be good. I think we'll have a nicer time than we did today. I'm sorry I skidded right into you in the supermarket. I often do stupid things like that.

Love Amy

P.S. Now you don't have to wait till your birthday to get a frame like this one!

57

# Chapter Nine

On Monday evening Amy and Sabrina's mum came back. It was so brilliant picking her up from the station. She hugged and cuddled Amy and Sabrina and gave their dad loads of kisses and cuddles in the car park, right in front of everyone. But Amy didn't care that people were watching them. It was so nice having her mum back.

On the way home in the car, Amy really wanted to talk to her mum, but

so did Sabrina and so did their dad.
And their mum had lots of news too.
The moment she'd finished telling them
all about the time when Granny got
cross with the postman for not pushing
the letters through the letterbox properly,
Amy started talking. "You know I told
you about the photo I sent to Hannah,
Mum?"

"Yes. Did she like it?"

"I haven't heard from her yet. Do
you think she will have got it? Dad said
it caught the last post on Friday."

"Er…where did you send it to? Her
mum's or her dad's?"

"Her dad's. Dad didn't know her
mum's address."

"Well, in that case, she might not
have got it yet."

That cheered Amy up a bit. But there

was a little voice that kept popping up inside her head and saying, Hannah doesn't like you, Amy.

On Thursday evening the phone rang. Amy's mum answered it, but she handed it straight to Amy.

"Hello," said Amy.

"Thank you for the present."

It was Hannah, and at the sound of her voice a lovely, relieved feeling came over Amy. "That's OK. Did you like the photo?"

"Yes, I love it. I only got it today. I've been at my mum's. Dad says he's going to make a copy of it and get me another frame, so I can keep one at my dad's and one at my mum's." Amy felt even happier because Hannah didn't sound all worried any more. In fact, she sounded really bubbly. And better still, she wanted to see Amy again. "Can you come to my dad's tomorrow?"

"I'll ask Mum. Hang on."

Amy's mum said yes straight away.

"There's not much to do here, though," said Hannah quietly.

"We'll think of something," said Amy.

"I can't wait," said Hannah in an excited voice. But then she suddenly sounded serious. "You're the first person to know about Mum and Dad splitting up."

Amy bit her lip. She didn't know what to say. She felt so sorry for Hannah.

"Well...my first *friend* anyway."

And then a lovely glow spread round Amy's whole body. "I can't wait till tomorrow," she said.

"Me neither," said Hannah.

And Amy smiled down the phone at her new friend.

# Make Friends with Jade

# Jade

## Ann Bryant

ORCHARD BOOKS

Cheltenham: 4 c
Acc No: 13313
Class:

*For Sue Mahon,*
*with grateful thanks for all your help*

ORCHARD BOOKS
96 Leonard Street, London EC2A 4XD
*Orchard Books Australia*
Unit 31/56 O'Riordan Street, Alexandria, NSW 2015
First published in Great Britain in 2002
A PAPERBACK ORIGINAL
Text © Ann Bryant 2002
Series conceived and created by Ann Bryant
Series consultant Anne Finnis
The right of Ann Bryant to be identified as the author
of this work has been asserted by her in accordance with the
Copyright, Designs and Patents Act, 1988.
A CIP catalogue record for this book is available
from the British Library.
ISBN 1 84121 794 4
1 3 5 7 9 10 8 6 4 2
Printed in Great Britain

Jade felt like a princess, with her low-cut neckline and her choker of yellow, white and gold flowers. She wanted to twirl around and around and around...

WITHDRAWN

Jade

# Chapter One

It was Friday afternoon. Everyone in the class was silent, waiting for the dreaded Maths marks. Jade was watching her teacher's face to see if she seemed cross or normal or happy.

"Well," began Mrs Tomkinson, in a stern voice, "I can't say that I'm thrilled about your Maths. Most of you made so many careless mistakes. You just rushed through it, instead of thinking about what you were doing."

Mrs Tomkinson let her gaze travel round the class. This was her way of telling everyone off. She just did it with her eyes. The class was used to it. In fact, as Jade looked round she could see that people were getting a bit fidgety, as though they were bored with the telling-off now, and wanted to get on with something else. But then Mrs Tomkinson's eyes stopped travelling round and landed on Jade.

Jade looked down. Her heart began to beat the teeniest bit faster and her cheeks turned the tiniest shade pinker. Please don't let her say that I've done really well.

"But as usual, there is one person, who's done some absolutely sooooooper work." Jade's heart banged against her ribs and she tried not to squirm in

her chair. She knew everyone was looking at her. She could just feel their eyes on her. Nasty, scornful eyes, because nobody likes a goody-goody clever clogs. "Well done, Jade. I'm giving you *two* stars, you did so well."

"Teacher's pet!" said Tom Dooley under his breath, from his desk just across from Jade's.

Jade felt her whole body going tense. Tom Dooley was the naughtiest boy in the class and he never tried hard in his work. Becky Barham was sitting next to Tom. She was one of Jade's friends, but she didn't tell Tom to be quiet or anything. There was a lump in Jade's throat.

"I wish you'd all take a leaf out of Jade's book," went on Mrs Tomkinson. She hadn't heard what Tom had said.

Jade was wishing Mrs Tomkinson would stop talking about the Maths and start on another topic. Because if she carried on, Tom might not be the only one calling her a teacher's pet. Sam Beeslee had once said it to her, and Jade was scared that it might spread round the whole class. Then everybody would hate her.

"Right, all come and sit on the carpet. Let's have a discussion about the weekend. I want to hear what exciting things you've got planned, all of you!"

Jade's spirits sank down to her socks because if she told the truth about what she was doing at the weekend, some people might think she was showing off. Being a show-off was as bad as being a teacher's pet. She sat near the back of the children on the carpet, hugged her

knees and bent her head over, trying to make herself as small as possible.

Then she began to say over and over inside her head, *Please don't let her pick me.*

# Chapter Two

"Right, let's start with you, Jade. I think you deserve to be first today."

Jade gulped. There was only one thing for it. She was going to have to tell a lie. She would pretend she was about to have the most boring weekend ever. She would say her parents were going away and Granny Mary was coming to look after her and her brother, Rory. Yes, that would be good, because Granny Mary didn't drive, so they wouldn't be able to

go anywhere. They'd just be stuck in the house the whole time. Maybe Jade would make up that Granny Mary didn't like them watching television or playing on the computer. Then surely everyone would feel sorry for her.

"Jade?" said Mrs Tomkinson. And Jade realised she'd been in a bit of a dream.

"Go on then, goody-goody," Tom whispered from just behind.

"What did you say, Tom?" asked Mrs Tomkinson sharply.

"Nothing, Miss," Tom answered, all innocence.

"Right, Jade. What are your plans for the weekend? Anything exciting lined up?"

"No," said Jade, trying to sound as though she was bored with even talking about it. "Mum and Dad are going away and Granny Mary's coming. It's

going to be awful, because she never
lets us do anything good..."

And then something terrible happened.
Jade had completely forgotten that she'd
told Becky what she was really doing at
the weekend.

"I thought you said you were going to
be trying on your bridesmaid's dress,"
piped up Becky. "For that wedding..."

Jade didn't know what to say now. All
she knew was that her face was very red.

"It's...it's been cancelled..." she
stammered.

"What? The wedding?" asked Mrs
Tomkinson anxiously.

"No, trying on the dress," said Jade,
not daring to look at anyone.

"Well I'm sorry to hear that, Jade," said
Mrs Tomkinson. Then she spoke in her
bright cheery voice. "But never mind, as

long as the wedding hasn't been cancelled, that's all that matters, isn't it? You're a very lucky girl, you know. How many of you others have ever been a bridesmaid?"

Nobody spoke.

"Well I remember when *I* was a bridesmaid," said Mrs Tomkinson, "many years ago. I wore a pink dress with layers and layers of petticoats and lots of lace and a very large bow. I absolutely loved it!"

Jade forgot about being upset for a moment because the lacy dress sounded so wonderful. She began to imagine herself wearing something like that at Helen's wedding.

"Pink petticoats! Yuk!" said a girl called Louisa under her breath. Jade heard though, and so did quite a few of the others.

Mrs Tomkinson didn't, thank goodness. "I bet you'll look as pretty as a princess, Jade," she went on.

"Teacher's pet," whispered Tom.

And Jade made an important decision at that moment. She was about to stop being such a good girl and start to be bad. She would purposely make lots of mistakes in her work and always be sure it was as scruffy as possible with plenty of crossing out and smudges. In fact, she'd make her whole self scruffier. And she'd start right now.

Jade looked at her neat white socks which were exactly level at the top, then she looked at Tom's socks. One was halfway up and the other was round his ankle. Very slowly, so no one realised what she was doing, Jade pushed one of her socks right down. Then she

14

pretended to scratch her head, but really she was pulling out her hairslide. It felt funny having her hair hanging over her face. She really wanted to push it behind her ear, but she didn't. She was also dying to pull her sock back up, but she made herself leave it, because this was the new Jade. A Jade with tatty hair and uneven socks, who thought pink petticoats were yuk.

# Chapter Three

"Would you believe it! My friend Helen getting married at long last!" said Jade's mum for the tenth time.

It was the next day, and they were in the car, going over to Helen's house.

"She's lucky," said Jade.

"Yes, but so are you! It's great that you've been chosen as one of the bridesmaids."

"Are the other two the same age as me?"

"I don't know. You'll soon find out, though!"

"What time are you going to pick me up, Mum?"

"Oh, Helen's going to drop you back about teatime, love. I can't wait to see what your bridesmaid's dress looks like."

Jade couldn't wait either. It was all so exciting.

"Hello Jade," said Helen, opening the door with a big smile on her face. "Come in and have a coffee, Lisa," she added to Jade's mum.

But Jade's mum was in a hurry to get back. "I'll see you later, love."

"Come and meet the others," said Helen to Jade, as she closed the front door.

Then there came a crash from somewhere in the house, followed by an

ear-piercing scream. Jade's eyes flew open.

"That'll be Sabrina!" said Helen, rolling her eyes. "She's the biggest pickle on this earth!"

A little girl with tangled hair and chocolate round her mouth came crashing out of the kitchen. Behind her was a girl of about Jade's age, with long straight hair.

"Give it back!" said the older girl. "Helen, she's nicked my chocolate." Then she stopped when she noticed Jade standing there.

"This is Jade," Helen said. "Meet my cousins, Jade! This is Amy and this is Miss Sabrina Picklekins!"

Sabrina let out a giggle, then ran into one of the downstairs rooms. A second later she reappeared.

"My name is Sabrina White, not

Sabrina Picklekins and I'm four years
and seven months old. So there!"

"My sister's a bit mad!" said the older
girl. "Just ignore her."

Jade thought Amy looked really cool
in her pale jeans and stripy T-shirt, with
nothing on her feet. She was swinging
on the bottom of the banister. It made
Jade feel suddenly girly and neat.

"Let's go and look at the bridesmaids'
dresses that I've chosen," said Helen.
"Your mums have told me your sizes,
but I can always exchange them if
they're not quite right." She began to
lead the girls up to the spare bedroom. "I
think you're going to like them. They're
a lovely lemon colour with enormous
sashes and loads of petticoats."

Jade thought the dresses sounded
beautiful. She threw a quick excited

glance at Amy. But Amy obviously
thought the dresses sounded disgusting
because she pulled a face. Immediately
a memory of that awful discussion on
the carpet came into Jade's head.
She mustn't act like a goody-goody.
She'd better agree with Amy.

"Yuk!" she mouthed, wrinkling her
nose.

Amy grinned.

Sabrina had rushed on ahead.

"Ooh! Lovely!" came her chirpy little
voice from the spare bedroom.

"Hang on a sec, chocolate chops!"
called Helen, racing after her with a tissue.

Amy suddenly climbed on to the
banister, slid all the way down, and
leapt back upstairs again two steps at a
time.

Jade wished *she'd* thought of doing

something like that, but she knew she
never would in a million years.

The dresses were lying on the bed
in cellophane wrappers. They looked
absolutely wonderful!

"What do you think?" asked Helen,
beaming.

Looking at her smiling face, Jade felt
like the most horrible person in the
world, for not answering straight away,
*Wow! They're so cool!* If only Amy would
say the first words.

At that moment, Sabrina picked up
both the bigger dresses and thrust one
of them at her sister and the other at
Jade. She only just managed to hold
them, they were so big compared to
her. "Put them on, you silly things!"

"Stop bossing everyone about!"
said Amy.

"I'm not. *You're* the bossy one!" said Sabrina, pouting.

"You two!" said Helen to Amy. "Why can't you be nice and quiet like Jade? I bet you don't argue with your brother, do you, Jade?" Jade felt her shoulders tensing up. *Nice and quiet* sounded so boring and goody-goody. And that was the last thing she wanted Amy to think about her. "Try them on then, girls," Helen went on. "Let me help you, Sabrina."

A couple of minutes later, Jade felt like a princess, with her low-cut neckline and her choker of yellow, white and gold flowers. She wanted to twirl around and grin and grin. But she couldn't. Amy would think she was pathetic. So she just stood there.

"A perfect fit!" smiled Helen. "And you both look gorgeous!" Then her smile

22

turned to a sort of sad frown. "What's the matter? You don't exactly seem over the moon, you two. Don't you like the dresses?"

Amy was looking at herself in the mirror. She caught Jade's eye and wrinkled her nose. Helen didn't see. "What's the matter?" repeated Helen. "Hm? Jade?"

Jade couldn't keep quiet any longer. Helen was waiting for her to say something. But what? Should she please Amy or should she please Helen?

"They're a bit kind of puffy," she stammered.

"Don't you like them, then?"

"Not all that much…"

Amy swung round. "Me neither," she said.

"Oh!" said Helen, taken aback. "I

thought you'd really love them... We can look at the catalogue and choose something else if you want."

"I think mine is lovely-lovely-lovely!" said Sabrina, dancing round the room.

"Be careful!" said Helen. "It doesn't look as though you're going to be wearing this one after all, Sabrina. We can't have the bridesmaids in different outfits from each other. I'll help you take it off while the others have a look through this."

She handed the catalogue to Amy and Jade who sat side by side on the bed. Jade was feeling awful.

"Wow! I like this!" said Amy, pointing to a picture of a dark blue silky all-in-one thing. It was sleeveless, had a tight top and went into flared trousers. The whole outfit shimmered and shone and

looked absolutely wicked. But Jade didn't think it was the kind of thing a bridesmaid should be wearing. It was more like something to wear at a disco. "It's so cool," Amy went on. "Do you like it, Jade?"

Jade hesitated.

"*Do* you like it?" Helen then asked her.

Jade gulped. "Yeah! Wicked!"

"OK then," said Helen. "You'd better take off those dresses."

Amy jumped off the bed and gave Helen a big hug. "Wow! Thanks, Helen. You're so nice."

Jade looked at Helen. She was smiling, but only just.

25

# Chapter Four

In the end it was decided that Jade and Amy would wear the blue outfits and Sabrina would still wear the yellow dress. Helen had laughed as she'd put the catalogue away, and said that she felt like an old fuddy-duddy because she wasn't up-to-date with what young girls liked to wear these days.

"It never occurred to me to let you two older girls wear something different from Sabrina," she'd added.

26

Jade thought about when her friend
Zoe had trapped her finger in the door
of her guinea-pig hutch and she'd not
even cried. Jade had told her mum about
it later and her mum had said that Zoe
must have been putting on a brave face.
Jade wondered if that was what Helen
was doing now.

After they'd finished talking about the
dresses and the flowers and everything
that was going to happen at the
wedding, Helen told Jade and Amy that
they could go outside for a while if they
wanted. "And *you*," she said to Sabrina,
"can come and help me make some
yummy chocolate buns!"

"Yes! Chocky buns!" said Sabrina,
jumping up and down with excitement.

It wasn't till Jade and Amy were
in the garden that Jade realised Amy

27

still had bare feet.

"Don't you mind about getting your feet dirty?" she asked.

"No!" said Amy. "What shall we do?"

Jade couldn't think of anything that would be exciting enough. There were daisies all over the grass, but Amy would probably think that making daisy chains was stupid and babyish.

There was the shed in the corner of the garden. "Shall we see what's in there?" she tried, hoping Amy would think it sounded like fun.

"Yeah!" said Amy, racing over, yanking the door open and disappearing inside. "It's mainly gardening things," she added, a few seconds later.

Jade hovered in the doorway, because she could see a few cobwebs and she didn't like spiders. There was a rusty nail

on the floor. She picked it up because she didn't want Amy to tread on it and hurt her foot.

"A nail!" said Amy, turning round at that moment. "I've got a good idea. We can scratch our names in the wood. Come on!"

Jade felt a bit anxious as she followed Amy round into the narrow gap between the back of the shed and the hedge. It was a tight squeeze.

It took Amy no time at all to scratch her name into the wood. She giggled as she handed the nail to Jade. "You'll probably be neater than me."

"No, I'll be really scruffy," said Jade. "What if Helen sees?" she couldn't help adding. The moment the words were out of her mouth she thought how goody-goody she must have sounded.

29

"Helen won't mind," said Amy. "We're not spoiling the shed, because we've done it on a bit that doesn't show."

It was true, Helen probably wouldn't see it at the back there. But all the same, Jade knew it was wrong.

Feeling really naughty, she started on the J. "I'm going to write Jazz," she said. "It's what all my friends call me." By the time she'd got to the second Z her heart had stopped beating quite so wildly and she found she was actually enjoying scratching the letters into the soft wood. She pressed herself back into the hedge so she could admire her handiwork.

"Told you yours'd be neater," said Amy.

Jade could have kicked herself. She'd forgotten about that.

# Chapter Five

"Did you remember to thank Helen?" asked Jade's mum as soon as she opened the front door.

Jade nodded and they both waved to Helen as she drove off.

"It was sweet of her to drop you off," her mum went on. "In fact it was very kind of her to have you three at her house for so long. I know *you're* a good girl, but I gather Amy is a bit of a tomboy and Sabrina is a little monster!"

Jade wished her mum hadn't said that. She thought back to the afternoon at Helen's. It had been good fun. It was true that Amy was a tomboy, but she and Jade had got on fine, and Jade was certain it was because she'd stopped being such a goody-goody.

"I'm not a good girl, Mum," she said firmly. Then her voice rose. "I wish everyone would stop saying that!"

"All right!" laughed her mum, putting her hands up in front of her face, as though Jade was a ferocious bear. "Let's change the subject. Tell me about the bridesmaids' dresses that Helen's chosen. Are they gorgeous?"

A guilty feeling came over Jade. She tried to push it away. "They're not exactly dresses," she began slowly.

Her mum's eyes widened. "Not exactly

32

dresses? What are they then? Skirts
and tops?"

"No, they're kind of trouser outfits.
Amy and I thought they were much
nicer than those puffy dresses with loads
of petticoats." Jade's mum was frowning.
Jade thought she'd better try to think of
something that her mum would like
about the trouser outfits. "They're dark
blue and really shimmery and silky.
We're going to feel like pop stars!"

The frown deepened on Jade's mum's
forehead. "And what's Sabrina wearing?"

Jade bit her lip. "Erm… She's wearing
an ordinary bridesmaid's dress, because
she's so little. It's yellow and it sticks out
a lot and it's got a big sash."

"I see," said Jade's mum in a tight sort
of voice. "And what is Helen going to feel
like walking down the aisle with one little

33

bridesmaid and a couple of pop stars?"

Jade and her mum had been standing in the hall all this time, but the hall felt suddenly too small to Jade.

"I'm hungry. Can I have a biscuit?" she asked, ignoring her mum's question and pushing open the kitchen door.

"We're having tea as soon as Rory's back from Mick's. And I believe I asked you a question, young lady."

Jade started flipping through the TV guide that was on the kitchen table, so that she didn't have to look at her mum.

"Helen liked the dark blue outfits," she said. But even as she was saying it, she wasn't sure if it was true.

"But did Helen actually choose them?" Jade's mum went on as she sat down at the table so she could look up at Jade's face.

Jade shut the TV guide and looked round for something else to do to avoid her mum's eyes.

"No, Amy and I chose them," she said, picking up the cat and stroking her.

"Mm…that's not like you. Are you sure you weren't just fitting in with what you thought Amy wanted?"

Jade buried her face in Cassie's fur. Then she suddenly looked straight at her mum. It was so annoying the way she'd guessed exactly what had happened. "No," she snapped, a bit more loudly than she'd meant to. Cassie jumped out of Jade's arms and ran away. "We both chose them because we didn't want to look like silly little girls." Jade scowled and stomped out of the kitchen. "So there!" she called from the hall.

# Chapter Six

On Monday morning Jade was dying
to show everyone that she'd changed
over the weekend. She wasn't a goody-
goody any more. Mrs Tomkinson usually
spent ten minutes after assembly and
before literacy hour with everyone
sharing weekend news. Jade was really
hoping she'd ask about her bridesmaid's
outfit. The girls would think a dark blue
shimmery trousery outfit was the best
thing ever. Even the boys might be

impressed. And when it was playtime Jade would tell Becky about how she and Amy had scratched their names on the shed. It would be so great if Tom got to hear.

"Right, everyone," said Mrs Tomkinson. "Funnily enough, *I'm* the one with some interesting news this morning!" She beamed round the room and spoke slowly and excitedly. "There's going to be a quiz for all the primary schools in our area, and we've got to choose one person from this class to be in our school team!"

Jade felt herself sliding lower in her chair and looking down at her desk. This was a terrible start to Monday morning. Any second now Mrs Tomkinson would say, "I think we'll have Jade!" And next thing Tom Dooley would be calling her

teacher's pet or goody-goody or something. And everyone would think, Oh no! Not Jazz Rawsthorne *again*!

"We ought to have Jazz," Becky suddenly called out.

"Yeah, Jazz," said several voices.

Jade stared at her desk. Becky had only said it should be her because it was obvious Mrs Tomkinson was going to choose her. She didn't want to look at anyone because she could just imagine the expressions on their faces – all scowly and fed up.

"Sooooper!" said Mrs Tomkinson. "That's all decided then."

She gave one last big beam to the whole class, then started on the literacy lesson.

Jade tried to settle down, but she felt too miserable to concentrate. Her eyes

wandered round. They happened to
rest on a pair of compasses on the front
table. She went back to her work, but
a few seconds later, she found herself
looking at the compasses again. And
that was when a great idea popped
into her head.

At the beginning of break Mrs
Tomkinson always sent the children
outside, then she went along to the
staffroom. A few minutes later she would
come back to check there weren't any
slowcoaches, as she called them, hanging
about in the classroom. Jade decided this
would be the perfect chance to show
Tom Dooley that she wasn't a goody-
goody or a teacher's pet – she was cool
and daring, and actually, quite naughty.

She smiled to herself and took another
look at the compasses. This time her

stomach suddenly filled up with butterflies. She wasn't sure if she dared to do it... What if the compasses didn't scratch the cupboard as well as the nail had scratched the shed?

"Right, pack away everyone," said Mrs Tomkinson as the bell for break sounded. "Anyone with a thesaurus, bring it to me. Dictionaries on this table, please. You'll need coats today."

Everyone started clearing their things away and going for their coats.

"I said dictionaries on this table, Tom. You don't listen, do you? Off you go, Sam, and remember, no eating snacks until you're in the playground."

Jade was clearing away as slowly as possible. Her fingers trembled, her stomach was still full of butterflies, and

she wished that Mrs Tomkinson would hurry up and go before Tom disappeared outside.

"I'll be back in a couple of minutes and I expect to find not a soul in the classroom," said Mrs Tomkinson, walking towards the door.

Jade waited a moment until only she and Tom were left in the classroom, then she turned to him and tried to sound excited. "I've got something to show you."

"What?" Tom looked bored.

"It's really good, honestly." Her heart thumping, she took the pair of compasses off the table and went round to the back of the cupboard. Tom followed her with a puzzled look on his face. Unfortunately, there wasn't enough room to squeeze between the back of the cupboard and the wall, so Jade decided she would have

to do it on the side, but down at the bottom, as near to the back as possible.

"Watch this!"

And she started to scratch the J of Jazz. It didn't feel at all the same as doing it with the rusty nail. The compass point would only make a thin line. Tom wouldn't be at all impressed. Jade gulped. There was only one thing for it. She pressed as hard as she could, scratching her name in really big spidery letters, doing it very quickly to get it over with.

The second she'd finished, she turned round. "There!"

Tom stood perfectly still, his eyes goggling and his mouth open. Jade's tummy turned a complete somersault inside her as she suddenly realised what she'd done. Her eyes flew back to the place where she'd scratched the cupboard,

and she wished more than anything in the world that she could wake up and find it was all a bad dream.

"What d'you do that for?" Tom asked her slowly.

Jade swallowed and spoke in a small voice. "I thought you'd think it was…" Then she stopped because it was all so embarrassing.

And that was when Mrs Tomkinson came back in.

"Come on you two slowcoaches. It's not like you to be the last out, Jade. I don't know what's got into you today."

Jade hung her head and followed Tom out.

# Chapter Seven

When Jade got home from school she went straight to her room. She kicked off her shoes, pulled off her socks, and changed out of her school uniform into her jeans and her only stripy T-shirt. Then she stood in front of the mirror. A second later a big scowl was covering her face. She wanted to be like Amy. She was wearing the same clothes as her, and she'd got nothing on her feet. She'd scratched her name in the classroom cupboard,

hadn't she? And yet it didn't seem to be working properly. The girl in the mirror still looked like the same old boring Jade.

She sighed a big sigh then went down to watch TV with Rory.

"What's the matter?" Rory asked her after a bit.

"Nothing," said Jade.

But it wasn't true. Her head felt like a washing machine, churning with worries.

"Why aren't you watching television properly then?" Rory asked.

"I *am*!" said Jade.

"No, you're not, you're just staring at it. What are you thinking about?"

And before she knew it, Jade had blurted out, "Helen."

"What about her?"

"Just about her wedding…and everything…"

Rory's eyes went back to the telly. He probably found Jade's thoughts boring. But Jade felt like talking now she'd started. When she and Amy had said they didn't really like the yellow dresses, Helen had looked so sad. Jade kept on remembering that moment. It made her feel terrible.

"I was thinking about what we're going to be wearing," said Jade, trying to get Rory to ask her some more questions. But Rory didn't say a word, so Jade tried harder. "Which do you think would look nicer, yellow or blue, Rory?"

"Uh?"

"Yellow or blue? Which do you think would look nicer?"

"It's not up to me, is it?"

Jade sighed. It was no good talking to boys about things like weddings. They

46

weren't really interested. And she couldn't talk to her mum and dad. She was already sure her mum thought she was being horrible to Helen.

"It's up to Helen," said Rory, his eyes glued to the telly. "It's *her* wedding, isn't it?"

Jade thought for ages about what Rory had said. It was true, it *was* up to Helen. She'd brought three beautiful dresses home and all Jade had said was that they were a bit puffy. Then they'd found the blue trouser outfits in the catalogue, and Jade had called them "wicked". Poor Helen.

For the next five minutes Jade couldn't get Rory's words out of her head. It's up to Helen. It's her wedding, isn't it?

The unfairness seemed suddenly too much to Jade. She jumped up and

BROOKFIELD
Brook Lane, Sarisbury Green
Southampton SO31 6DU

went into the kitchen.

"Can I phone Helen, Mum?"

"Helen? What about?"

"To tell her I've changed my mind about the bridesmaids' outfits. I like the yellow dresses that she chose much better than the blue things. I don't care what Amy thinks."

Her mum gave Jade a big smile. "Yes, of course you can use the phone, sweetheart. Give Helen my love."

When Jade rang off from talking to Helen, she felt a strange mixture of relieved and worried. Helen had sounded really happy and said it wasn't too late to change. But then Jade had suddenly got worried and asked what Amy would think. Helen had said it didn't matter what she thought, because now two out

48

of three bridesmaids wanted to wear the dresses, and Helen *definitely* preferred them. So that was it. Decision made.

# Chapter Eight

It was just after assembly on Tuesday morning, and Jade knew something was wrong. Mrs Tomkinson was at her table, sitting very still. Her eyes were travelling slowly round the class and she wasn't smiling. Jade's heart began to beat more and more loudly. This was it! A big telling-off was about to happen. Any minute now the whole class would be staring, gobsmacked, at Jazz Rawsthorne.

But Jade didn't want to be told off.

50

She felt awful. She should never have done such a terrible thing. Even Tom Dooley had looked at her as though she was completely mad.

"Somebody," began Mrs Tomkinson, in a low slow voice, "has scratched the name Jazz into the side of my cupboard."

Some leaves were blowing against the wall outside. They sounded really noisy compared to the silence in the classroom.

"Well?" said Mrs Tomkinson in her angriest voice. "I'm waiting…"

And then Jade got a big shock, because a voice from across the classroom said, "It was me, Miss."

Jade couldn't help gasping. Everyone looked in Tom's direction. He went a bit pink. Why was he being kind to Jade, taking the blame for something that wasn't his fault? He didn't even like her.

He thought she was a teacher's pet. Everyone stared at him as he squirmed around in his seat.

Screwing up all her courage, before she could change her mind, Jade blurted out, "It wasn't Tom. It was me, Mrs Tomkinson."

The class all swung their heads round the other way to look at Jade now. She could feel their eyes boring into her.

"Are…are you sure, Jade?" said Mrs Tomkinson, frowning.

Jade nodded.

Then Tom spoke again. "No, it was me. Jazz is only saying it was her to get me out of trouble."

Jade couldn't believe her ears. All eyes were back on Tom. Mrs Tomkinson coughed. "Well I must admit, I never imagined that *two* people would own

52

up…" Her eyes kept darting up to the ceiling, as though there might be something written there, telling her what to say next. She suddenly put on a very strict I'm-in-charge voice. "I've got some furniture polish here. The pair of you can spend your break time polishing the whole cupboard. It won't get rid of the scratches, but it might help, and the cupboard could certainly do with a polish. I don't know whether one or both of you is responsible for this dreadful vandalism, but I never want to see such a thing in my classroom again. Is that clear?"

"Yes," said Jade softly.

Tom just nodded hard.

The class was very quiet for the next hour and a half. Jade didn't look at anyone, but she could feel people looking at her.

When it was break time Mrs Tomkinson gave Tom and Jade each a rag and some polish, then left them to it.

As soon as she'd gone out, Jade turned to Tom. "Why *did* you say you'd done it, Tom?"

"Dunno," said Tom, working hard.

They both rubbed away in silence for a while. But Jade's head was buzzing with questions. She tried again.

"But I don't get why you said you'd done it..."

Tom rubbed even harder.

Jade waited a few seconds, then tried again. "So...why did you?"

"I dunno...'cos...'cos...I felt sorry for you 'cos I li—"

He suddenly broke off, bent down and polished the bottom of the cupboard harder than ever.

Jade wanted him to finish the sentence. "What were you going to say?"

"Don't talk, then we'll get it done faster."

So not another word was spoken till they'd finished the job. Then Jade just said, "Thank you."

"'S OK," said Tom, as he raced off outside.

When Jade went into the playground, Becky came rushing straight over to meet her.

"Why did you say *you* scratched the cupboard, Jazz? We don't get you."

"Because it *was* me," Jade answered.

Sarah and a few other girls came over then.

"Jazz *did* scratch her name on the cupboard," Becky told them importantly.

"Why?" asked a girl called Louise.

Jade looked round the group of girls. Every one of them had kind eyes. It made her suddenly want to tell them even more of the truth. "I thought I'd do something naughty, to stop people thinking I'm a goody-goody."

Becky put her arm round Jade. "We don't think you're a goody-goody," she said.

"'Course we don't," the others agreed.

"Tom does," said Jade softly.

"No he doesn't," said Sarah. "He really likes you. I know he does, because I heard him tell my brother you were cool, and he went all red when he said it."

Jade's eyes flew open. It seemed like she'd got everything wrong. She looked across the playground at Tom. He was in the middle of getting told off again; this time, by Miss Norgrove, the teacher

on duty. Jade watched him as he hopped from foot to foot, kicking the ground so the dust in the playground made a little cloud round his ankles.

A moment later the telling-off was over and he strolled off to find his mate, Sam. On his way across the playground he noticed Jade looking at him, and gave her a big friendly grin.

"*See!*" said Sarah. "I'm right, aren't I?"

Jade suddenly knew what Tom had been going to say in the classroom.

"Yes, I think you're right," she said, grinning back at Tom.

# Chapter Nine

On the morning of the wedding Jade arrived at Helen's house before Amy and Sabrina. By the time they turned up, she was already in her dress and choker.

Amy stopped in the doorway. "Wow! You look lovely, Jade!" she said, her eyes wide. "I'm going to look awful compared to you."

"And I'm going to look the prettiest of you all!" piped up Sabrina, pushing past Amy to get to her little dress that

was lying on the bed.

Both girls laughed but Jade still felt a bit anxious.

"I thought you might be cross when Helen told you we were changing back to these dresses. You see, I felt sorry for her when I got home…"

"Me too. I didn't like them at first but when I saw myself in the mirror with it on I thought I looked really nice. I only pretended not to like the dresses because I didn't want you to think I was all girly."

And that was when Jade knew she had nothing more to worry about. She could just enjoy Helen's wedding.

Walking down the aisle beside Amy and behind Helen and Sabrina, Jade felt like a princess. She thought it was probably the best moment in her life.

But an even better moment came just after the big reception meal. Amy had gone out into the hotel garden and Jade was just about to join her.

"I made you this," said Amy, rushing in to find Jade. She handed Jade the most beautiful daisy chain. "You don't think daisy chains are silly, do you?" she asked anxiously.

"No, I love them," said Jade, putting it round her neck. "I'll make one for you, shall I?"

"No, because I know I wouldn't look as nice as you. I've been trying to look like you ever since I met you, and I can't. I've been trying to act like you too. You're so much more sensible than me."

"I'm not, honestly."

"You are."

Jade couldn't believe what she was

hearing. Into her head came a picture of Tom Dooley, eyes wide, mouth open, staring at what Jade had done to the classroom cupboard.

And just then Helen appeared. She put one arm round Jade and one round Amy and said, "How are my two princesses? Scratched your names anywhere good lately?"

Jade's heart started beating faster and Amy went a bit red. Helen waltzed off in her beautiful silky white dress.

Amy and Jade exchanged a guilty look then noticed that Helen had turned round. She was grinning at them. "Don't worry, it will always remind me of my two gorgeous bridesmaids and this wonderful day," she called, giving them a wink.

When Jade looked at Amy she saw

that she'd gone bright pink. "Come on, Amy. I *am* going to make you a daisy chain."

Amy smiled and followed Jade outside.

Coming up next in...

# Make Friends With
# Amy

**Amy's got the perfect photo opportunity –
and she's going to take it!**

flip me over!

# Who will YOU meet next?

Make Friends With books are available from all good bookshops,
or can be ordered direct from the publisher:
Orchard Books, PO BOX 29, Douglas IM99 1BQ
Credit card orders please telephone 01624 836000
or fax 01624 837033
or e-mail: bookshop@enterprise.net for details.

To order please quote title, author and ISBN
and your full name and address.
Cheques and postal orders should be made payable to
'Bookpost plc.'
Postage and packing is FREE within the UK
(overseas customers should add £1.00 per book).

Prices and availability are subject to change.

# Make Friends With

1. **Chloe ★ Jessica**    1 84121 734 4    £3.99 ☐

2. **Georgie ★ Megan**   1 84121 784 0    £3.99 ☐

3. **Lily ★ Izzie**    1 84121 786 7    £3.99 ☐

4. **Claire ★ Lauren**    1 84121 790 5    £3.99 ☐

5. **Yasmin ★ Lucy**    1 84121 792 1    £3.99 ☐

6. **Rachel ★ Zoe**    1 84121 794 8    £3.99 ☐

7. **Jade ★ Amy**    1 84121 796 4    £3.99 ☐

8. **Hannah ★ Poppy**   1 84121 798 0    £3.99 ☐

Look out for...

# Make Friends With

# Hannah

How will **Hannah** track down her
new-found friend?